who u 2?

Steve Barlow & Steve Skidmore
Illustrated by Geo Parkin

Created by Telefónica O2 UK.

o2.co.uk

Published by Telefónica O2 UK Limited,
260 Bath Road, Slough SL1 4DX, UK.

ISBN 978-0-9561419-0-3

First published 2009.

10 9 8 7 6 5 4 3 2 1

Printed and bound in the EU on paper approved by the Forest Stewardship
Council. Products carrying the FSC label are independently certified to assure
consumers that they come from forests that are managed to meet the social,
economic and ecological needs of present and future generations.
www.fsc.org

✉ who wnts 2 no?

Zip and Mouse were walking home when a high-pitched beeping sounded from Mouse's school bag.

Is that your mobile?

Mouse read the screen and groaned. "It's only Dud. He's bugging me again with one of his stupid messages. He can be such a *WOMBAT* sometimes."

"WOMBAT?" Zip raised his eyebrows. "You mean he's a cuddly, Australian marsupial?"

"No, he's a Waste Of Money, Brains and Time."

"Oh, that sort of *WOMBAT.*" Zip peered at Mouse's phone:

"Not again!" said Zip. "Dud's always finding dodgy sites. Let's check it out."

"Your wish is my command!" Mouse tapped at the keypad and seconds later the homepage of **WeAreGonnaMakeYouRich.com** appeared.

"He must be joking!" exclaimed Zip. "We'd better get round to his house and see what sort of trouble he's getting himself into this time."

Mouse sighed. "I suppose so. I'll just let Mum know where I'm going." She began to text, her thumbs blurring across the keypad:

Hi M, OMW 2 C M8. BBL. HAND, TTFN M

She pressed SEND. "Come on, then, let's see what daft Dud's found now."

They were on Dud's front door step when the return message came:

Mouse rolled her eyes. "She is such a dinosaur. Look, she even uses *apostrophes! In a text message!* She just doesn't get the wonders of technology. She'd be happier with a postcard, or a carrier pigeon. I get blisters every time I have to text her…"

I said, Hi Mum, on my way to see a mate. Be back later. Have a nice day, ta ta for now. Mouse

The answer came almost immediately:

OK. B gd. Ma

"Oh, very hip." Mouse put her phone away as the door opened.

"Oh well that proves it," said Mouse, sarcastically. "It *must* be all right."

Dud gave Mouse and Zip a wink. "*Exactly!* Come on in, dudes, and marvel!"

Dud's bedroom looked like an explosion in a recycling plant. Clothes, soft drinks bottles and fast food cartons were scattered all over the floor and, in the case of stickier items, the walls.

Mouse swept a tottering pile of pizza boxes off a chair and sat down. "I just *love* what you've done with this place."

Zip pointed at Dud's computer. "I'll never understand why your mum and dad let you keep that in here."

"Where else is there to keep it?" asked Dud.

"In the family room, where everyone can see what's going on."

"You are so sad," replied Dud. "My mum and dad don't care what I look at."

Mouse glanced across at Zip and shrugged.

Dud plumped his bottom into a swivel chair and span around to face his computer screen.

"So what's this great site you've found all about?" asked Zip.

Dud made '*shush'ing* motions with his hand and began to read: "'We have a few questions to check whether you are the sort of person we can help.' Okay, guys, bring it on.

'Question One: Do parents, guardians or other responsible adults keep an eye on what you do on the internet?'" Dud grinned. "Hah! Fat chance!" He typed NO. "Question Two: 'Are you of an intelligent and inquiring turn of mind?'"

"I know the answer to that one!" Mouse waved her hand in the air. 'It's '*No*'!"

Dud scowled at her. "I was going to say '*Yes*', you made me type '*No*' by mistake! Shut up, I'm trying to concentrate! Right, last question. 'Do you believe everything anyone tells you?' He stabbed at the keyboard, saying each word of his answer out loud as he wrote it: '*I cer-tain-ly do.*' There!" He leaned back. A clock face appeared on the screen with the message:

Then the screen changed. A banner opened, balloons floated around, champagne bottles popped their corks, magic wands shot out bursts of stars and another message appeared:

"*Yes!*" Dud punched the air and danced around the room. "Yes, oh yes! *He shoots, he scores!*"

Mouse gave him a disgusted look. "What are you gibbering about? And what's this website that's so great you drag us over here to see it?"

Dud pointed at the screen.

Mouse read the URL. '*WeAreGonnaMakeYouRich.com*'? What do they do?"

Dud peered into Mouse's eyes and said, very slowly,

They... Make... You... **Rich!**

Mouse snorted. "Why would anybody want to make *you* rich? It sounds too good to be true. What's in it for them?"

"D K, D C," said Dud. "Don't know, don't care. I just wanna be rich."

Zip frowned. "It sounds like a scam to me."

Dud glared at him. "Do you think I'm a *complete idiot?*"

"Of course not," said Mouse. "You're missing too many parts to be a *complete* anything."

"I'll have you know I'm nobody's fool."

"Only because you can't find anybody to adopt you."

"Oh, *har har.*" Dud punched at keys. "The site's legit. I checked it out on Thikipedia."

THIKIPEDIA

'What can I tell you?'

We AreGonnaMakeYouRich.com

From Thikipedia, the free encyclopedia

> THIS ARTICLE DOES NOT CITE ANY REFERENCES OR SOURCES. PLEASE HELP IMPROVE THIS ARTICLE BY ADDING CITATIONS TO RELIABLE SOURCES. UNVERIFIABLE MATERIAL MAY BE CHALLENGED AND REMOVED.

WeAreGonnaMakeYouRich.com is a totally real, genuine site that gives loads of money away to deserving young people and it's not a cover for horrible slimy aliens who want to suck your brains out through your ears, honest.

"See?"

Zip stared at Dud. "That doesn't prove anything! What about the *WARNINGS?*"

"What *WARNINGS?*"

"It's a free-access site. Anyone could have put that information up there - it doesn't mean to say it's *true!* All that stuff about '*no references or reliable sources*' is telling you that nobody's checked the article."

"All right then." Dud was getting annoyed. He punched at keys. "You want more proof? Take a look at this."

Myouterspace Webchat

At 15:37 PM **Dangerous Dud** joined the room

15:37 PM **Roger**: Our triumph is at hand! Soon rest of fleet will arrive & then Earth is ours *ahahahahahaha-haha!*

The messages above were sent before you arrived. To send a private message, type <nameofuser> your message here:

SEND

Mouse said, "You call yourself *Dangerous Dud?* More like *Der-brain Dud.*"

Zip stared at the screen. "*'Earth is ours?'* I don't like the sound of that."

Dud didn't look up. "It's just chat stuff. Probably a role-play game or something. Watch this." He sent a message:

"hi guys. got sum stiffs here who thnk wearegonnamakeyourich.com is a con."

He clicked on 'send'.

Far above, Dud's message was intercepted by
an alien spaceship hanging menacingly in orbit
around the Earth. In the ship's control room,
a communications officer looked up from his
station. "Captain, sir. An incoming message…"

25

Myouterspace Webchat

15:40 PM **Tim**: Hi, Tim here! That's right,
Lord Skullsplitter of the Vhrrrlx, I mean
Roger, I'm definitely not an alien, I don't
suck other creatures' brains out through
their ears, not even a little bit, and
www.wearegonnamakeyourich.com is really
good.

15:40 PM **Roger**: It certainly is, we have
both had lots of lovely money from this very
genuine and worthwhile site and we are
now rich beyond our wildest dreams.

SEND

"See? I told you it was legit." Dud logged off
the Myouterspace site with an air of triumph.

Mouse gazed at Dud in wonder. "How did you get so stupid without special training? There's something very dodgy about all this."

Another message appeared on the computer screen:

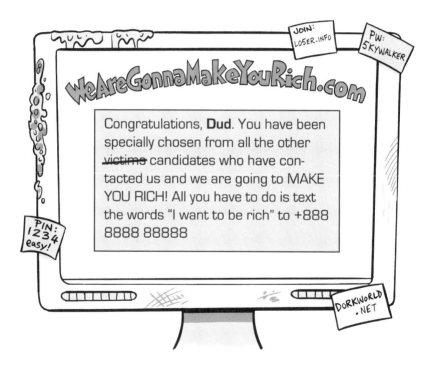

Dud reached for his mobile.

Mouse grabbed his wrist and pulled his hand away from the phone. *"Don't do it!* You've no idea how much this is going to cost, and if you text them, they'll have your mobile number."

"So?"

"So, jellybrain, you should *NEVER* give your number to anybody you don't know."

"You worry too much." Dud snatched his phone up and sent the message.

Moments later, a reply arrived:

"Thank you, Dud. You will soon be rolling in untold wealth! Please send us a photograph for identification purposes."

"Hold on!" Zip was horrified. "If you send them a photo, they can do *anything* with it! They could send it to websites with names like The World's Ugliest People or Incredibly Weird Pets. It could be out there on the internet forever!"

But Dud ignored him. He ran a comb through his hair, then selected the camera function on his phone and held it at arm's length.

"Zip's right," said Mouse as the shutter clicked. "Anyway, you're not supposed to post offensive pictures on the Net."

"I'm only sending a picture of *me!*"

Mouse glanced at the picture of Dud on the screen. "I'd call that pretty offensive…"

Dud sent the picture. Then he stuffed
the phone into his top pocket.

"Captain!" said the communications officer, "I have traced the primitive Earth-phone signal to its source."

"Good." The Captain rubbed his mandibles together. "As soon as we have a picture, I can send the snatch squad in. Then it's brain-sucking time. Has everybody got their straws?" Grinning, the crew waved their brain-drinking straws. "Excellent!"

"Picture coming through now, sir." The communications officer stared at his screen and pulled a face. *"Yeeeuch!"*

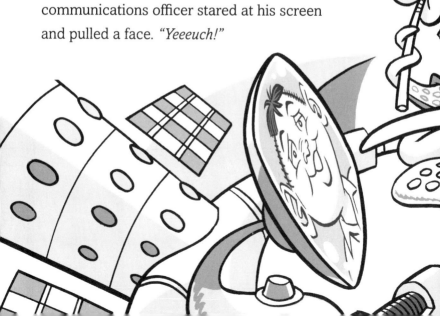

"Whoa!" Mouse looked daggers at Dud. *"Don't you dare tell them.* It's bad enough giving out your own details to someone you don't know – giving out other people's is a serious *no-no.*"

"I'm not telling them which school I go to," said Dud indignantly.

"Good," replied Mouse. "I'm glad you're seeing sense at last."

"Why should those creeps at school get loads of money from the site I found? I hate them. They call me a geek and they hide my shoes." Dud clicked on the REPLY button. He typed, *'No way, Jose'*, and clicked on SEND.

Sad faces appeared on the screen.

"Okay, okay." Ignoring Zip and Mouse's protests, Dud sent the school address.

Mouse folded her arms and glowered at Dud. *"You shouldn't have done that."*

The Captain chortled as Dud's message arrived. "Now, all we have to do is search their Internet for the details of their school…" The Captain licked his lips, his nose and his eyeballs.

Dud immediately began to type his address into the box.

"Grab him!" yelled Mouse. *"Sit on his head!"* Between them, Zip and Mouse wrestled Dud to the floor. "He's not just out to lunch: he's out to lunch, dinner, supper and a late night kebab on the way home from the pictures!"

"Gerroff!" screeched Dud. "Are you crazy? I'm that close to getting my hands on *a fortune!"*

"Listen," said Zip. "I don't know what's going on here – all that stuff about not being slimy aliens and sucking brains out, why even mention that if it's not true? I mean, yes, it's pretty weird, but it's no weirder than people you don't know giving you money. *Don't tell them your address. You don't know what might happen.*"

"I know what'll happen if I don't – *I'll be poor!*" With a burst of superhuman strength, Dud flung off his captors and clicked on SEND.

For a few moments, Zip, Mouse and Dud sat on the floor glaring at each other. Then the doorbell rang.

Dud dusted himself off with dignity. "If you've quite finished being weird and violent," he said, "I will go and answer the door. And if it's my money being delivered, don't think you're getting any." He marched out of the room. Mouse and Zip exchanged helpless glances.

Back in Dud's room, Zip was looking through the window. "Mouse," he said slowly, "what's big and green and slimy and alien looking?"

"A big green slimy alien, I should think. Why do you ask?"

"Because four of them are carrying Dud off to something that looks like a spaceship."

Zip ran his fingers through his hair. "We've got to help him!"

"Why?"

"Because they're probably going to suck his brains out!"

Mouse looked puzzled. "And we should be concerned about this, because…?"

"Well, I don't think they'll be content just with Dud's brain, do you?"

Mouse considered. "I suppose not. It must be very small."

"And if they like his brain - maybe they'll want to *suck everyone's brains out!*"

"That would not be a good thing. *What do we do?*"

Zip thought for a moment. "I've got an idea. He's still got his phone, hasn't he?" Mouse nodded. "All right." Zip took his phone out and keyed in Dud's number.

The Captain grinned a nasty alien grin. "Don't worry, human, this won't hurt much."

"You're going to suck my brains out," screeched Dud, *"and you're telling me it's not going to hurt much?"*

"Oh, it's going to hurt you an awful lot! But I promise you I won't feel a thing." The Captain raised his drinking straw and winked at his squirming victim. "Ready or not, here I come!"

The Captain halted, his straw mere centimetres from Dud's left ear. "What is that noise?"

His First Officer saluted. "I believe it is the human's primitive Earth-phone, sir."

"Oh…right…er, should I answer it, do you think? It might be important." The captain reached into Dud's pocket and took out his phone. "Er…how does this work?… ah, got it, got it!" He pressed the ANSWER button.

"Hey, Dud, is that you?" squawked the phone.

The Captain drew himself up into an imposing state of blobbiness. "Certainly not! This is Lord Skullsplitter of the Vhrrrlx…" The Captain realised that his crew were all making frantic tentacle signals for him to shut up: he covered the phone and hissed, "What?"

"Stop fooling about doing alien voices, Dud, I know it's you," said the phone. "How's the plan coming along?"

The Captain was baffled. "What plan?"

"Come on, you know what plan. Have you finished destroying the aliens yet?"

The Captain exchanged appalled glances with his crew. "What do you mean?"

"I said, have you destroyed the aliens?" said Zip. "With that plan of yours when you bravely volunteered to let yourself be captured and infect them with that deadly virus…" Inspiration ran out and he gestured urgently to Mouse.

"The virus," said Mouse, thinking quickly. "The one that our top scientists injected into your brain… The virus that's harmless to humans but *deadly to aliens…*"

"Yes, that's the one," went on Zip. "We just wanted you to know that we're really impressed that you're giving up your brain, such as it is, for the sake of the whole planet and…" He held out the phone at arm's length and looked at it. "They rang off."

A moment later, a spaceship *hurtled* out of the sky at an *unimaginable speed* and landed in the street. A door slid open, and Dud appeared. Something that looked very like a boot connected forcibly with his backside, and he flew through the air to land at Zip and Mouse's feet.

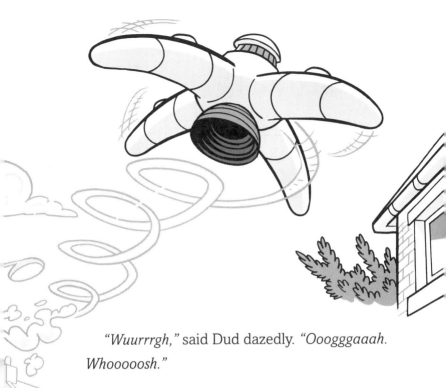

"*Wuurrrgh,*" said Dud dazedly. "*Ooogggaaah. Whooooosh.*"

Mouse regarded him critically. "Do you think the aliens have sucked his brains out?"

"Maybe," said Zip. "How would we tell?"

"They didn't," said Dud in a shaking voice. "They were going to, but after the Captain got that phone call he said they couldn't find any, so *they let me go!*"

The aliens get to work. They set their snares all over the World Wide Web and the mobile phone networks.

But what unwary victim will fall into their terrible traps?...

Handy tips for avoiding
brain-sucking aliens:

1.

Never give your personal details or photo out over the phone or internet to someone you've never met before.

2.

Don't believe everything that's written on the internet. There's a lot of rubbish out there.

3.

If in any doubt about the offer, don't trust it. The aliens are getting smarter and smarter all the time.

"Reading is a skill for life, and literacy has never been more important than now, in the digital age.

We want this book to inspire your children to read for enjoyment, but it also has a more serious message. In the online world, children can find themselves at risk from unwanted contact, inappropriate behaviour and potentially harmful content.

Technology is available to help keep children safe, but is only part of the solution. It's also important that children learn how to be smart and stay safe as part of their own online experiences.

By introducing children to the Cybernuts, we hope to make their digital adventures safer... and much more fun."

Ronan Dunne, CEO, Telefónica O2 UK